To Gigi and Sammy.

Library of Congress Cataloging-in-Publication Data available.

ISBN 978-1-4521-8338-1

Manufactured in China.

Design by Sara Gillingham Studio.
Handlettering by Sergio Ruzzier.
The illustrations in this book were rendered in pen, ink, and watercolor.

10 9 8 7 6 5 4 3 2 1

Chronicle books and gifts are available at special quantity discounts to corporations, professional associations, literacy programs, and other organizations. For details and discount information, please contact our premiums department at corporatesales@chroniclebooks.com or at 1-800-759-0190.

Chronicle Books LLC
680 Second Street
San Francisco, California 94107

Chronicle Books—we see things differently.
Become part of our community at www.chroniclekids.com.

THE SLEEPOVER

and Other Stories

chronicle books·san francisco

CONTENTS

THE SLEEPOVER

KNOCK KNOCK.

It's me: Chick!

Hi, Chick. What are you doing here? It's late.

What do you call it when someone goes to a friend's home to sleep over?

A sleepover.

Right!

Let's have a sleepover.

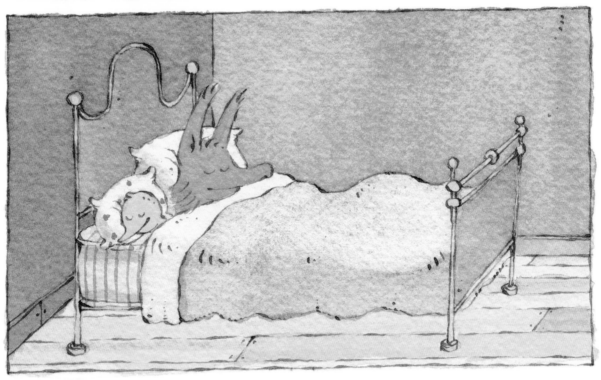

Fox?

Yes,
Chick?

Are there kangaroos
around here?

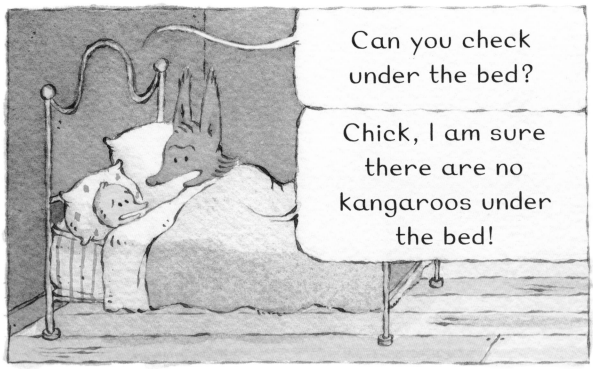

Kangaroos are very good at hiding. Can you please check?

Okay, Chick, I checked. There are no kangaroos under the bed.

Can you check inside the closet?

Why are you worried about kangaroos, Chick?

I would hate being eaten up by a kangaroo.

I don't think kangaroos eat chicks, Chick.

Of course they do.

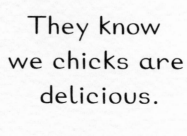

They know we chicks are delicious.

Chick, can we sleep now? It's very late.

Fox, I need to get Rupert.

Who is Rupert?!

I cannot sleep
without Rupert.

Chick!
What's that?!

Oh, don't be
afraid, Fox.

This is Rupert,
my stuffed
kangaroo.

. . .

Goodnight, Fox.

THE HAMMER

What do
you do with
a nail in a
wall, Fox?

You can hang something on it.
A painting, perhaps.

Yes, I will make a
painting and hang it
on that nail.

31

THE SURPRISE

Don't worry, Fox.
I will forget you are
throwing me a party.

Alright, Chick.
Come back this
afternoon.

Why should
I come back this
afternoon, Fox?

Please come back later, Chick.

I like my sprinkles pink and round.

You are spoiling your surprise birthday party!

You are right, Fox. I will come back this afternoon.

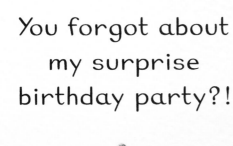

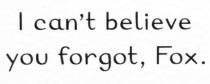

41

Oh, Fox. You did remember!
Chocolate cake!
Pink, round sprinkles!
No party hats!

This is the first and
best surprise birthday
party I have ever had.

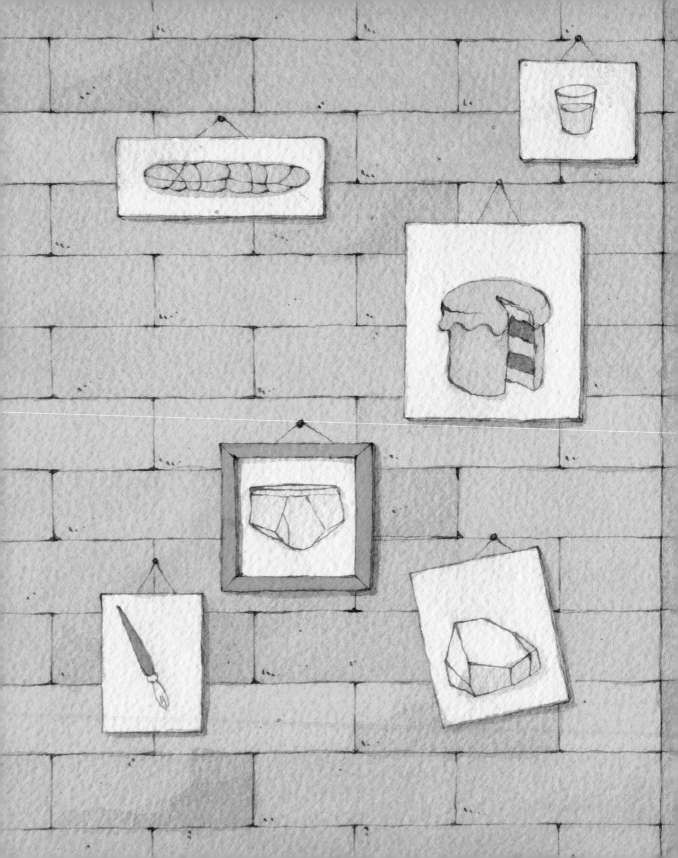